Can I Have a STEGOSAURUS, Mom?

Can I ?
Please!?

by Lois G. Grambling
Pictures by H. B. Lewis

Troll Medallion

Can I have a Stegosaurus, Mom?
Can I?
PLEASE!?
If I had a Stegosaurus, Mom . . .

My Stegosaurus could sleep with me
in my bed every night,
and I wouldn't have to worry about scary monsters
jumping out of my closet
and pouncing on me
as soon as I close my eyes.

'Cause if they ever even tried,
my Stegosaurus
would jump out of my bed
and pounce on them.
And they'd be squashed.
SPLAT!
FLATTER THAN FLAT!

Can I have a Stegosaurus, Mom?
Can I?
PLEASE!?
If I had a Stegosaurus, Mom . . .
When you made some yucky vegetable for supper
and put tons of it on my plate
and said I couldn't have any dessert
until my plate was clean,
my Stegosaurus
could eat it all up
for me.
And my plate would be sparkling
clean!
And you'd be happy.
And I'd be happy.
And my Stegosaurus would be happy, too.
'Cause a Stegosaurus really loves yucky vegetables.
Ms. Frosser told us that
in science class.

And if Ms. Frosser
forgot to reserve the school bus
for us
the day we were supposed to take
our field trip to the museum,
my Stegosaurus could take us.

And I'd sit high on his head
with Ms. Frosser.
And the other kids could sit
up and down
the rest of him.

And I'd tell Zelmo Zimmer
to hold on tight
to the spikes
on his tail
so he wouldn't fall
off.
(Ms. Frosser ALWAYS seats us
alphabetically!)

Can I have a Stegosaurus, Mom?
Can I?
PLEASE!?
If I had a Stegosaurus, Mom . . .
Whenever there was a parade in town
I'd get the best view of anyone.
'Cause I'd climb up
on my Stegosaurus
and see everything!
And the drum major
would wave at me
as he passed by.
And I'd wave back.

Can I have a Stegosaurus, Mom?
Can I?
PLEASE!?
If I had a Stegosaurus, Mom . . .

At summer camp
my Stegosaurus and I
would do GREAT
in all the races.
Thundering across the finish line.
First!
Every time!
And . . .
we'd do GREAT
in the Tug of War,
too!
The kids on the other side
wouldn't have a chance!

Can I have a Stegosaurus, Mom?
Can I?
PLEASE!?
If I had a Stegosaurus, Mom…

On Halloween
you and Dad wouldn't have to go out
trick or treating with me.
My Stegosaurus would.
And I'd be safe!
Really safe!
Who'd pick on a little Stegosaurus
trick or treating
on Halloween
when a BIG STEGOSAURUS
was with him?

AND . . .
Who wouldn't give a special treat
to a little Stegosaurus
ringing their doorbell
on Halloween
when a BIG STEGOSAURUS
was with him?

Can I have a Stegosaurus, Mom?
Can I?
PLEASE!?
If I had a Stegosaurus, Mom . . .
My Stegosaurus would make
a super mascot
for my peewee football team,
cheering us on
during half time.
And . . .
thundering
up and down the bleachers
every time
anyone
made a touchdown!
The crowd would go wild!
And so would the coach!

Can I have a Stegosaurus, Mom?
Can I?
PLEASE!?
If I had a Stegosaurus, Mom . . .
And I suddenly remembered on Christmas Eve that I'd
left something off my Christmas list,
I'd jump on my Stegosaurus
and we'd go galloping
galloping
galloping
to the North Pole.
FAST!

And when we got there
I'd tell Santa what it was
I left off my list.
And Santa would thank me
for coming.
And he'd add it to my list,
of course!
BUT, Mom . . .

THE MOST IMPORTANT REASON
for having a Stegosaurus . . .
the one that REALLY counts the MOST, Mom . . .

Is that
yesterday
I found this
GIGANTIC
egg
in the woods
under a pile of leaves,
and I've been sitting on it
ever since.

And
it's beginning to crack open
right NOW!
Crack!
CRACK!!
CRACK!!!

UH-OH!!

Can I have a Tyrannosaurus Rex, Mom . . .
Can I?
PLEASE!?
If I had a Tyrannosaurus Rex, Mom . . .

To my sons, Jeff and Mark.
L.G.

For Mom and Dad,
Something to share with
Nicky and Carly.
H.B.L.

Text copyright © 1995
by Lois G. Grambling.
Illustrations copyright © 1995
by H. B. Lewis.

Published by Troll Medallion, and imprint and
trademark of Troll Communications L.L.C.

First published in hardcover by BridgeWater
Books.

Printed in the United States of America.

10 9 8 7 6 5 4 3 2 1

Library of Congress Cataloging-in-
Publication Data

Grambling, Lois G.
Can I have a Stegosaurus Mom? Can I?
Please!? / by Lois G. Grambling; illustrated
by H. B. Lewis.

p.   cm.

Summary: A child describes all the possible
advantages of having a Stegosaurus for a pet.
ISBN 0-8167-3386-4 (lib.)
ISBN 0-8167-3387-2 (pbk.)
[1. Stegosaurus—Fiction.   2. Dinosaurs—
Fiction.]   I. Lewis, H. B., ill.   II. Title.
PZ7.G7655Can   1995   [E]   93-39178